Francis Close

The tendency of church principles, so called, to Romanism

Antigonos

Francis Close

The tendency of church principles, so called, to Romanism

Reprint of the original.

1st Edition 2024 | ISBN: 978-3-38601-357-4

Antigonos Verlag is an imprint of Outlook Verlagsgesellschaft mbH.

Verlag (Publisher): Outlook Verlag GmbH, Zeilweg 44, 60439 Frankfurt, Deutschland, info@outlook-verlag.de
Vertretungsberechtigt (Authorized to represent): E. Roepke, Zeilweg 44, 60439 Frankfurt, Deutschland
Druck (Print): Libri Plureos GmbH, Friedensallee 273, 22763 Hamburg, Deutschland

THE TENDENCY

OF

"CHURCH PRINCIPLES,"

SO CALLED,

TO ROMANISM:

PROVED AND ILLUSTRATED FROM THE RECENT PAMPHLET OF

REV. WILLIAM PALMER, AND FROM DR. HOOK'S

"CHURCH DICTIONARY."

BY REV. F. CLOSE, A.M.

Incumbent of Cheltenham.

SECOND EDITION—SECOND THOUSAND.

London:

HATCHARD AND SON,

HAMILTON, ADAMS, AND CO.

1843.

CHELTENHAM : PRINTED BY J. J. HADLEY,

Journal Office, Queen's Buildings.

THE
TENDENCY OF "CHURCH PRINCIPLES,"

SO CALLED,

TO ROMANISM.

A candid acknowledgment of "EXISTING TENDENCIES TO ROMANISM," in the bosom of our Church, in the heart of a leading University, among its most distinguished Scholars, Tutors, Divines, and Professors—and this from the pen of one of themselves,—himself one of the most learned, cautious, and withal amiable and conciliating of their number, is an event of no common interest to the Church, and affords a testimony which must be valid in the estimation of all parties. The Rev. William Palmer, the friend and associate of Mr. Froude, Mr. Newman, and Dr. Pusey, and an eye witness of the Theological movement at Oxford, from its commencement, has been reluctantly compelled by conscientious feelings to record, and to condemn in the strongest manner the secession of some, and the tendency of others of his friends, associates, or disciples, to secede to the Roman Apostacy. In the execution of this painful duty he has depicted with great force the extent of these wide spreading evils—and with every disposition not to exaggerate them he has described a state of things calculated to awaken and alarm every friend of *Protestant Principles*, whether within or without the pale of the Church of England.

Those who have from the beginning been opposed to his theological system have often been censured as alarmists, because they ventured to predict the events which Mr. Palmer now so justly deplores—they with him must now lament the fulfilment of their own predictions.

The object of Mr. Palmer's Pamphlet* which has just appeared, is to rescue himself and certain others of his friends from the responsibility, and I might justly add, the *guilt* of having occasioned this fearful inroad upon the safety of our Church. Attributing the Romanizing tendencies of some of his friends to other causes, he endeavours to show as well by a narrative of facts, as by a statement of his views, that these deplorable defections have not been occasioned by the Theological opinions of himself and some of his associates, which opinions he calls "CHURCH PRINCIPLES." He reasonably concludes that the public at large will be led to connect these defections with his "*Church Principles ;*" a term so prominently avowed, so tenaciously held, so perpetually harped upon by the party in question ; and he sets himself to the task, confessedly difficult, of disconnecting these lamentable results, from what would seem to be their natural and immediate cause :—he labours " to clear those who uphold *Church Principles* from the imputation of approving certain tendencies towards Romanism." At this point then we join issue :—and it is confessedly the object of the following pages to prove the converse of his proposition, viz.: that what this respectable writer denominates " *Church Principles,*" are the original and fruitful source of all those " uncouth consequences" (as Bishop Hall would have called them) which have followed each other in rapid succession.

But in order that we may keep in view the magnitude of the question debated, let me pause here for a moment, and place before my reader Mr. Palmer's own description of the present tendencies to Romanism within the pale of the Church ; in fact in connexion with the very persons whom he labours to uphold and defend.

" Within the last two or three years," he observes, " a new school has made its appearance"—

He should rather have said a new race of *scholars* has sprung up,— we shall find that the *school* is the same ; though the disciples may have outrun their teachers.

* " *A Narrative of Events connected with the publication of the Tracts for the Times, &c.*" By the Rev. Wm. Palmer, A.M. of Worcester College, Oxford. Parker, Oxford.

" The Church has unhappily had reason to feel the existence of a spirit of dissatisfaction with her principles, of enmity to her Reformers, of recklessness for her interests.

" We have seen in the same quarter a spirit of—almost *servility* and *adulation* to Rome, an enthusiastic and exaggerated praise of its merits, an appeal to all deep feelings and sympathies in its favour, a tendency to look to Rome as the model and standard of all that is beautiful and correct in art, all that is sublime in poetry, all that is elevated in devotion. So far has this system of adulation proceeded, that translations from Romish rituals, and ' *Devotions*' have been published, in which the very form of printing, and every other external peculiarity, have evinced an earnest desire for uniformity with Rome. *Romish Catechisms have been introduced, and form the models for similar compositions.*

" In conversation remarks have been sometimes heard, indicating a disposition to acknowledge the supremacy of the See of Rome, to give way to *all its claims*, however extreme, to represent it as the conservative principle of religion and society in various ages; and in the same spirit, those who are in any way opposed to the highest pitch of Roman usurpations are sometimes looked on as little better than heretics. The Gallician and Greek Churches are considered unsound in their opposition to the claims of Rome. The latter is held to be separated from *Catholic* unity. The ' See of St. Peter' is described as the centre of that unity ; while our state of separation from it is regarded, not merely as an evil, but a sin—a cause of deep humiliation, *a judgment for our sins !* The blame of separation, of *schism*, is unscrupulously laid on the English Church ! *Her reformers are denounced in the most vehement terms.* Every unjust insinuation, every hostile construction of their conduct is indulged in ; no allowance is made for their difficulties, no attempt is made to estimate the amount of errors which they had to oppose. Displeasure is felt and expressed if any attempts are made to expose the errors, corruptions, and idolatries approved in the Roman communion. *Invocation of saints is sanctioned in some quarters ; purgatory is by no means unacceptable in others ; images and crucifixes are purchased, and employed to aid in private devotion.*"

This in the bosom of a *Protestant* University !

" *Celibacy of the clergy—auricular confession, are acknowledged to be obligatory. Besides this, intimacies are formed with Romanists, and visits are paid to Romish monasteries, colleges, and houses of worship.* Romish controversialists are applauded and complimented ; their works are eagerly purchased and studied ; and contrasts are drawn between them and the defenders of the truth, to the disadvantage of the latter. The theory of development advocated in the writings of De Maistre and Möhler (Roman Catholic controversialists), according to which the *latest* form of Christianity is the most perfect, and the superstitions of the sixteenth or eighteenth century are preferable to the purity of the early ages, is openly sanctioned, advocated, and avowed. In fine, *menaces* are held out to the Church, that if the spirit which is thus evinced is not encouraged, if the Church of England is not '*unprotestantized,*' if the Reformation is not forsaken and condemned, it may become the duty of those who are already doubtful in their allegiance to the Anglo-Catholic communion, to declare themselves openly on the side of its enemies." (pp. 44, 45.)

Then he adds—

" I have no disposition to *exaggerate* the facts of the case; *all who have had occasion to observe the progress of events will acknowledge the truth of what has been said.*"

In page 49 he continues :—

" It is now admitted on all hands, that there is a tendency to Romanism in some quarters. The author of Tract 90 stated, that his object was to keep certain persons from ' *straggling in the direction of Rome.*' Dr. Pusey has written at some length on the ' *acknowledged tendency* of certain individuals in our Church to Romanism! Difficult *as it has been for Churchmen to realize to themselves the strange and almost incomprehensible fact, that any who had ever professed Church principles should have a tendency to Romanism, they have been gradually and reluctantly compelled to admit the lamentable truth. Actual secessions from the Church, few, indeed,*"——

Few, indeed! We may unhesitatingly affirm that there have been more secessions from the Church of England during the last ten years than there had been in the previous fifty, or perhaps one hundred! Eight or ten clergymen of our Church have publicly gone over to Romanism; several under-graduates have followed them; while not a few of the students of both our universities have become deeply tinged with popish principles—this is indeed " *sufficiently alarming!*"——

" A change of tone in private society; and above all, the doctrine continually and systematically advanced in the ' British Critic' can leave no further doubt of the existence of the evil."

And at the close of his 4th chapter he acknowledges that the present perils of the Church occasioned by this school of divines, are as imminent as they were in 1833, when the revolutionary principle threatened her destruction.

"The dangers which now threaten us, are not inferior to those which surrounded the Church in 1833; the tendency to latitudinarianism has been replaced by a different, but not less dangerous tendency; while the spirit of disaffection to the Church has only taken a new form. It seems, therefore, a *plain duty* to hold out some warning to those who might be in danger of being deceived."[*]

These, then, are the tremendous results which must have proceeded from some adequate moving cause. What that cause may be is now the subject of our investigation. Mr. Palmer solemnly abjures the idea of any approximation towards Rome; and he argues that his Church Principles could never lead him in that direction. With this object, he traces the history of the Oxford movement from its commencement to the present time. He states, that in the year 1833, an attempt was made by himself and his friends to form an Association in Oxford, in defence of the Church—their simple object being to arouse her friends to a sense of the dangers which threatened her, and to promote a combination in her favour. It is not necessary to my present argument to follow him through the various methods, which in common with others, he adopted to promote these objects—nor to examine the degree of success which attended their efforts. Although not a few persons will be surprised to find Mr. Palmer and his associates taking credit to themselves for some combinations in defence of the Church at that period which certainly originated from independent

---

[*] This alarming description of the present state and prospects of our Church (resulting in some way or other from the Oxford movement) is singularly inconsistent with another picture drawn by the same hand at p. 87 of this same pamphlet. " In conclusion, it is impossible not to advert in a spirit of deep thankfulness to the prospects of the Church, and the progress of Christian principles and practice. *Who shall say that much has not been done within the last ten years?* And what may we not humbly expect from the blessing of God on patient, and humble, and persevering endeavours for personal and general improvement? *A Theology deepened and invigorated;* a Church daily awakening more and more to a sense of her privileges and responsibilities; a Clergy more zealous, more self-denying, more holy; a laity more interested in the great concerns of time and eternity; Churches more fully attended; sacraments and divine offices more frequently and fervently partaken; unexampled efforts to evangelize the multitudinous population of our land, and to carry the word of God into the dark recesses of Heathenism." Mr. Palmer appears to take the credit of these improvements to himself and his friends. He must take the dangers and perils which have been created by his party along with them. " The deepened Theology," together with " the Romish tendency and disaffection to our Church." And we can only say—" *Doth a fountain send forth at the same place sweet waters and bitter?* "—James iii. 11.

sources. But contemporaneously with these measures, a much more influential plan was struck out by some of Mr. Palmer's associates, and actually commenced, during his temporary absence from the University. The celebrated series of *Tracts for the Times* commenced in the autumn of the same year, 1833. Of the character and tendency of these tracts, Mr. Palmer appears to have stood in doubt from their very commencement. " I received these tracts which were published during my absence, and aided in their distribution at first, because their general tendency seemed good; though I confess I was rather surprised at the rapidity with which they were composed and published, without any previous revision or consultation." (p. 21.) During the autumn and winter of that *same year*, Mr. Palmer resolved on totally disconnecting himself from those publications, to which, in fact, as an author, he never contributed. He continued to watch their progress—and, as we gather from his pamphlet—his disapprobation of them increased. He perceived, " that the " Theology of the non-jurors, was exercising a very powerful influence " over the writers of the tracts."—" Some of " us felt deeply uneasy on witnessing such questionable doctrine " mingling itself with the salutary truths which we had associated " to vindicate"—they "were driven to the verge of despair."—"*Several* " *leading friends of Church principles, such as Dr. Hook, and Mr.* " *Percival*, felt themselves obliged at last publicly to announce their " dissent on various points." (pages 24, 25.) Yet partly from love to the individuals, and partly from approbation of the greater portion of their writings, Mr. Palmer and others who thought with him, preferred bearing the imputation of sanctioning what they did not approve, than by an open secession to endanger a disruption of the party with whom they acted. Their situation was doubtless sufficiently embarrassing.

"We endured much of what we could not approve—exaggerated views of the independence of the Church ; undue severity to the Reformers ; too much praise of Romish offices ; a depreciating tone in regard to our own ; not to speak of views on ' Sin after baptism,' the ' doctrine of Reserve,' and other points which were more than questionable : but we were satisfied that the imputation of Romanism was *really* unjust and unfounded ; and therefore we could not assume any hostile position." (p. 43.)

At length, however, the extravagancies of some of the party reached such a height, that Mr. P. could not conscientiously remain silent; —and seeing among his friends and their disciples, not only tendencies to Romish doctrine, but actual secession to that communion, he could forbear no longer, and the result is his present pamphlet; in which, while he exposes the deplorable consequences of these pernicious, writings, he endeavours to rescue the more sober of his friends from the unenviable charge of originating them.

"The evil has been distinctly perceived for more than two years by some friends of Church principles, who have been withheld from taking any decided and open step in opposition, by the apprehension lest such a proceeding might have the effect of precipitating events which they would deeply deplore. It seems, however, that there is *more danger* in continuing silent, when we perceive the increasing dissemination of most erroneous and decidedly Romanizing views, under the assumed name of Church principles, and when the advocates of those principles are universally *identified* with doctrines and practices which they most strongly disapprove." (p. 49.)

It is only justice to Mr. Palmer to state, that he is far more anxious to rescue his " Church Principles," than himself from the imputation of Romish tendencies. Speaking of himself and his associates, he says—

" That any tendency to Romanism should ever exist amongst *themselves*; that Church principles should ever become the path to superstition and idolatry; that they or their disciples should ever become alienated from the English Church, never entered their imaginations as possible. When their opponents charged them with such tendencies, the charge was always steadily denied. They availed themselves of every opportunity to clear themselves from the imputation of Popery. They even contended against the errors of Romanism. They had no intention to assist in the propagation of those errors." (p. 38.)

Yet most important admissions are made in page 46, though accompanied with renewed protestations against Romanism.

" *I will not say that the writers of the Tracts have not been, in any degree, instrumental in drawing forth this spirit; I will not inquire how far it is traceable to the publication of Froude's ' Remains,' and to the defence of his views contained in the Preface to the second series of the ' Remains:' nor will I examine how far it* may be a reaction against ultra-Protestantism : it is unnecessary now to enter on this painful and complicated question, on which different opinions may be entertained. One thing, at least, is most perfectly certain : it never was the *intention* of the advocates of Church principles to promote Romanism : they have always been persuaded that their principles do not, by any fair and legitimate reasoning, lead to that system, to which they have ever been conscientiously and firmly opposed; and I am persuaded that they will feel it a duty to offer to the Church every possible pledge of their attachment to her doctrines ; that if their names have been employed to sanction any system which generates a spirit of dissatisfaction with the English Church, and tends to the revival of Romish errors and superstitions, they will adopt such measures as may be sufficient to mark their disapprobation of such a system, and their sense of its inconsistency with the principles which they maintain." (p. 46.)

Mr. Palmer will, however, acknowledge, that those who dread the inroads of Popery into. our Church, had some grounds for alarm, and some reason to connect the recent Romanist demonstrations with the Oxford party, when he himself asks how, under recent circumstances, they could rescue themselves from the charge ?

" But what can we say—what defence can be made, when it is undeniable that ROMANISM, IN ITS VERY FULLEST EXTENT, HAS ADVOCATES AMONGST OUR-SELVES ; that they have influence in the ' British Critic ;' THAT THEY ARE ON TERMS OF INTIMACY AND CONFIDENCE WITH LEADING MEN, that no public protest is entered against their proceedings by the advocates of Church principles." (pp. 69, 70.)

I have thus endeavoured as fairly as I can in a sketch necessarily brief, to glean from Mr. Palmer's pamphlet his *historical argument*, if I may so call it, by which he endeavours to prove his point. I will not stop to enquire here how far all the consequences of the publication of the Tracts, and even of the more broadly erroneous treatises, reviews, &c. with which the press has teemed during ten long years, are chargeable on one who all the while was sensible of the errors promulgated, yet as far as the public is concerned continued his sanction, and lent his respected name to the hurtful cause—or how far his present measured and qualified condemnation, even of Tract 90 tends to redeem the mischief which has been occasioned ; I have no desire to be the censor of Mr. Palmer or of any individual, but I must deeply lament that he did not sooner proclaim his misgivings to the Church and to the world, and that his present disruption with acknowledged error is not more bold and decisive.

Viewing the movement as thus far developed, I suspect that few who are not as strongly wedded to a system as Mr. Palmer himself has been, will be disposed to withhold their conviction, that whatever " Church Principles" may be, the present wide spread diffusion of Romanism must be laid at the door of many who profess those Church Principles.

In 1833, when the Oxford movement commenced, no one had ever heard of the smallest inclination towards Rome in the Clergy or Laity of the Church of England, much less in the Students of our Universities. The public mind, as Mr. Palmer justly shows in his pamphlet, was moving in an opposite direction—and the bare possibility that in the space of ten years there should be such an extended inoculation of Romanism as now exists had occurred to no one. This wide spread inundation of error will and must be traced to Oxford—to Mr. Palmer and his associates. The protestation of innocence of purpose (for which I give Mr. Palmer full credit) will avail nothing against facts that cannot be gainsaid nor refuted. Principles were gradually developing themselves, detected by some from the beginning, lamented —feebly opposed, and but by a few; allowed to gather strength, and ascendancy; until it is now but too evident that a demon has been raised who refuses to be laid, and a fire has been kindled (unintentionally I trust) which cannot easily be extinguished. It is impossible to disconnect the various parts of the whole Oxford Theological movement—it has proceeded step by step, even by Mr. Palmer's own showing, until it has reached the present climax; and now Mr. Palmer in retiring from the arena, hopes not only to deliver his own conscience, but to rescue his " *Church Principles*" from the condemnation in which they appear likely to be involved. This effort will I hope prove futile. I am sure Mr. Palmer neither thinks nor believes that his principles on Church matters, have any tendency towards Rome—*but he may be mistaken*—and one would almost hope that with such bitter fruit in his hands as these principles have already yielded, he may himself be convinced that there must be some nascent tendency to essential Romanism in them. This question I will proceed further to argue. The historical evidence is conclusive thus far, *that Romanism as it now exists within and without the English Church has proceeded from those distinguished men at Oxford who profess these " CHURCH PRINCIPLES."*

But the reiterated assertion again returns upon us that Church Principles never could produce, nor ever had a tendency to produce such results. This awakens an anxious enquiry—What are " *Church Principles?*" a phrase occurring in almost every page of Mr. Palmer's pamphlet! I turn to his chapter devoted to that topic, and I confess myself unable to glean from it any definite ideas on the subject, and I am constrained to look elsewhere for a definition of " Church Principles." As far as my own experience goes, I find hardly two persons agreeing in any explanation of the term, and I am therefore driven to the writings of some accredited author for information. This I find in a work published by the Rev. Dr. Hook of Leeds. Mr. Palmer, as we have seen, refers to him as "a leading friend of Church Principles,"* and one who was early offended at the Romanizing tendency of the Tract writers or their associates: and Dr. Hook in the work alluded to, repeatedly cites " the learned Mr. Palmer;" they thus mutually accredit each other; and in taking Dr. Hook's *Church Dictionary,* as authority in deciphering the enigma, " What are Church Principles?" I am surely occupying ground which must not only afford a fair field of investigation, as far as the Oxford movement is concerned, but must also be most unobjectionable to Mr. Palmer himself.†

The spirit in which Dr. Hook's Church Dictionary is composed differs widely from that which is displayed in the pamphlet of his friend Mr. Palmer; and in producing Dr. Hook's opinions I hope I shall not catch

---

* Foot-note page 25.

† I wish to add here that when I read Mr. Palmer's recent Pamphlet, I had never seen Dr. Hook's " *Church Dictionary;*" (though I may have occasionally met with an extract from it) and that the idea of referring to it as a standard of *Church Principles* was suggested to my mind exclusively by Mr. Palmer's laudatory reference to him.

anything of the asperity in which he too often indulges towards those to whom he is opposed.

In citing this peculiar authority on the subject of "Church Principles," special advantage is afforded me, because of the vast variety of ecclesiastical topics, and doctrinal subjects, on which the Dictionary peremptorily decides; while the very nature of the work itself renders me less liable to the charge of perverting or exaggerating the author's meaning.

The student who searches for authority upon this important subject in Dr. Hook's work, should bear in mind these two points—*first*, that the author explicitly disavows all those errors of Romanism which he conceives to be of *modern date;* and *secondly*, that in every article where he cites the authority of the "*Primitive Church*," and "*the antient Church*," he does so *with approbation*—the Church of the third and fourth centuries being his model of ecclesiastical excellence both in doctrine and discipline.*

The first important point which we shall investigate is the nature of the Sacrament of the Lord's Supper as viewed by the light of "Church Principles." To elucidate this point we must refer to the words " *Altar* "—"*Priest* "—" *Sacrifice* "—" *Viaticum.*"

" ALTAR.—The place on which gifts or sacrifices to God are offered in religious worship. As since the foundation of the world we know but of one sacrifice acceptable to God, and beneficial to men, for its own sake, even the sacrifice of Jesus Christ ; so in this high and strict sense we know but of one Altar, even the Cross on which the Lamb of God himself, both Priest and Sacrifice, was offered for the sins of the world." (p. 15.)

Thus far well: but it is the style of the writers of this School, first to state truth in terms to which none can object, and then to *qualify* or encumber it in a subsequent paragraph, in such a manner that the force of the original position is broken and lost. Thus he adds :—

---

* See under " *Primitive Church*," page 454.

" But as in the Church of God before our Lord's coming there was an altar on which were offered, by God's ordinance, gifts and sacrifices, *prefigurative* of that upon the Cross : so in the Church of God since the Lord's coming there is an altar on which, by His appointment, are offered gifts and sacrifices *commemorative* of that upon the Cross. The table of Holy Communion, or Lord's Table, in the Christian Church is therefore called an altar, because on it are placed in presentation before God, the appointed memorials of the Lord's Body and Blood; and because on it are also offered the alms of the faithful worshippers. See our Lord's directions to his followers on this point, (Matt. v. 23.) and St Paul's declaration (Heb. xiii. 10.") (p. 15.)

Yet in no part of our *present* accredited liturgics, or Church offices, can Dr. Hook produce a single instance of the term *Altar*, applied to the Communion table in the English Church!* He attaches, however, great importance to the term and to the thing signified by it; and in the pages which follow he gives a history of *stone altars*, which arose " in the earliest ages of the Church." (p. 17) and *therefore* in his view the purest : the early Christians solemnized the rites of their faith in catacombs, whither they were driven by persecution—and in sacred spots—they often built tombs on the place where the martyrs died, which served as the altar of a Christian Church.

" Afterwards, perhaps, a more magnificent edifice was erected over the same spot, and the tomb of the martyr remained in the crypt, while the altar was raised immediately over it; *access to the crypt and its sepulchral monument being still permitted to the steps of the faithful."*

The tendency to superstition in the minds of the "common people" in connexion with stone altars, occasioned the necessity of their removal at the Reformation; "but," says, the author, "we cannot look with " indifference on those few examples of the original stone altars still " remaining, which witness to us of an almost universal custom for " several centuries."

These altars being established, we must next be furnished with *sacrificing priests.* So under the head of "Priests," (p. 452) while

---

* Here, as in other places, he cites obsolete canons and Royal ordinances, not binding on us, in support of his views.

the plain doctrine of Rome is denied—viz. "that of a true propitiatory "sacrifice for the sins both of the living and the dead,"—and the thirty-first Article cited to refute it—the following observations occur :—

"At a period very ancient, the whole of Divine worship was distinguished by the title of *Sacrificium*, or sacrifice. This name was given to the prayers and praises, preaching, and devotion of body and soul to Christ, in the Sacraments of Baptism and the Lord's Supper. But more particularly, and with greater dignity, was the term applied to the consecrated symbols of the Body and Blood of Christ, called by St. Chrysostom "the tremendous sacrifice." The ministers officiating were also endowed with the corresponding title of "priests," *(sacerdotes,)* and Bishops had the appellation of "*summi sacerdotes*," (chief priests.) And these names were given, not with relation solely to the administration of the Eucharist, but to the exercise of their prerogative in the various acts of Divine worship. It was one act of the priest's office to offer up the sacrifice of the people's prayers, praises, and thanksgivings to God, as their mouth and orator, and to make intercession to God for them. Another part of the office was in God's name to bless the people, particularly by admitting them to the benefit and privilege of remission of sins, by spiritual regeneration in Baptism. Above this was *the power of offering up to God the people's sacrifices at the altar ;* that is, as Mr. Mede and others explain them, first the *eucharistical oblations of bread and wine* to agnize or acknowledge God to be the Lord of the creatures ; then the sacrifice of prayer and thanksgiving in commemoration of Christ's bloody sacrifice upon the cross, mystically represented in the creatures of bread and wine ; which whole sacred action was commonly called the *Christian's reasonable and unbloody sacrifice,* or *the sacrifice of the altar.*" (p. 452, 453.)*

So again, under the head of "Eucharist" (p. 262), the same character is attributed to the elements in the Lord's supper.

"As *the bread and wine* which our Lord distributed at the institution of His supper, *was part of the paschal feast,* or *sacrifice of the Lord's passover,* and as such had first *been offered in sacrifice to God,* it is clear that unless His ministers first offer, *in sacrifice to God,* the *bread and the wine* which they distribute at the Lord's supper, *they are not fulfilling their Lord's command,* and they are not doing as He did. Hence the Lord's Supper has always been considered *a sacrifice as well as a sacrament ;* a thanksgiving memorial presented before God, as well as a means of grace to men. The Lord's Supper, *in respect of the oblation or pure*

---

* The italics in this paragraph, and in many others, are *mine :* intended to draw attention to particular expressions.

offering of bread and wine therein presented before God, was foretold by the prophets as the worship which would be offered to God throughout the world, by the Gentiles on their conversion to Christianity. (See Isaiah, xix. 19, 21 ; Malachi, i. 11.)

But the most objectionable statements upon this subject occur under the head of " *Sacrifice ;*" (pp. 502-504), and are not Dr. Hook's own, though cited as authority by him.

" Sacrifice.—An offering made to God on His altar -by the hand of a lawful minister. *In strictness of speech* there has only been one sacrifice once offered and never to be repeated, the sacrifice of the death of our Lord Jesus Christ. He suffered death upon the cross for our redemption, and made there, by His one oblation of Himself once offered, a full, perfect and sufficient sacrifice, oblation, and satisfaction for the sins of the whole world. *(See Satisfaction.)* Figuratively speaking, all Divine worship was anciently called a sacrifice : our sacrifice of prayer and praise. But more especially was the term applied to the celebration of the Holy Communion. As on this latter subject much misunderstanding has prevailed, the following remarks are transcribed from the late Archdeacon Daubeny's Guide to the Church. ' St. Paul tells us (Heb. xiii. 10), that we have an altar* in the Christian Church. If so, we must have a *sacrifice* and a *priest*, for these are correlative terms.

" ' In conformity with this established idea, the primitive writers often called the Lord's table an altar, and the holy Eucharist an altar offering, before it became the Lord's Supper; *and the holy table*, like the altar at Jerusalem, they considered to be used *as an altar for sacrifice,* before it was employed as a table for a sacrificial feast ; the holy elements being consecrated and offered up as a *commemorative sacrifice,* in which is *represented* before God the sacrifice of Christ upon the cross, in consequence of which solemn office of the priest, they become the Body and Blood of Christ in spirit and effect to all faithful receivers. It follows, then, unless the Church has been under a great mistake upon this subject from its first establishment to the present time, that when there is *no priest* there can be *no sacrifice,* and when there is *no sacrifice,* there can be *no receiving* of the Body and Blood of Christ ; for the elements must be first made Body and Blood by consecration, before they can be received as such by the congregation.'—' And who,' says the learned Hickes, ' but a priest can receive the elements from the people, and offer up to God such solemn prayers and thanksgivings for the congregation, and make such solemn intercession for them, as are now, and

---

* The extraordinary perversion of this allusion of the Apostle's must strike most readers !

ever were, offered and made in this holy Sacrament ? *Who but a priest can consecrate the elements by solemn prayer*, and MAKE THEM THE MYSTICAL BODY AND BLOOD OF CHRIST ? *Who but a priest can stand in God's stead*, and *at His table*, and in *His name, receive His guests?* Who but a priest hath power to break the bread and bless the cup, and make a solemn memorial before God of His sufferings, and then deliver his sacramental Body and Blood to the faithful communicants, as tokens of His meritorious sufferings and pledges of their salvation ? *A man thus authorised to act for man in things pertaining to God, and for God in things pertaining to men, must be a priest, and such holy ministrations must be sacerdotal, whether the holy table be an altar, and the Sacrament a sacrifice or not.*"

The Archdeacon may well start a little at his own language here—and fear lest the people should " give him credit for the least tincture of Popery," but he quiets their fears by assuring them that " this was the language used in the Primitive Church," and therefore could have nothing to do with Popery ! This is a perpetually recurring but most fallacious argument of the Divines of this school—who appear to think that because the usurpation of the Popedom did not occur until centuries later, that therefore the foundations of the errors on which that superstructure was subsequently erected could not have been laid in the third and fourth centuries ! St. Paul, however, declared even in his day that " the mystery of iniquity, did already work"—and here is the point of the whole argument !

The Archdeacon, however, complacently affirms, " such is the " idea which *our Church* entertains upon the subject—she considers the " Sacrament of the Lord's Supper to be a feast upon a sacrifice : to " constitute it such, that which is feasted upon, must have been first " *made a sacrifice, by having been offered up by a Priest ! !*"

That our Reformed Church affirms no such thing—whatever *the Primitive Church* may have done, is most evident from the extraordinary effort which Dr. Hook has made to prove that she does so, and the signal failure that must overtake that attempt. Under the head of " *Oblation*," (page 401,) we read as follows :—

" In the office for the Holy Communion we pray God to accept our alms and oblations. The word oblations was added to this prayer for the Church militant here on earth, at the same time that the rubric enjoined, that if there be a communion, " the priest is then," just before this prayer, " to place upon the table so much bread and wine as he shall think sufficient." *Hence it is clearly evident that by that word we are to understand the elements of bread and wine, which the priest is to offer solemnly to God,* as an acknowledgment of His sovereignty over His creatures, and that from henceforth they may be peculiarly His."

How severely pressed must our author have been to find a shred of authority for his views in the writings of our Church, when he was led into so palpable an error as this !

If the term " *Oblation,*" here refers to the elements of bread and wine, how does it happen that the *side Rubric* directs that " if, there be " no alms or oblations, then shall these words be left out unsaid ! !" Dr. Hook himself in the following two pages, gives the real meaning of the word " *Oblations ;*" shewing that they were originally pecuniary offerings for the Priest himself. If this is all the authority in " our Church," which Dr. Hook and the Archdeacon can cite for their views upon the priestly oblation of the sacrifice of the altar, and a feast upon it, the members of the Church of England may feel confident that if such are the " *Principles*" of any " *Church,*" they are not the " *Church Principles*" of that " pure and Reformed part of " Christ's Holy Catholic Church established in these realms !"

But under the word " *Viaticum,*" we find assertions relative to the Eucharist even more perilous. I give the passage entire :—

" VIATICUM, the provision made for a journey. Hence, in the ancient Church," (and therefore the pure Church) " both Baptism and the Eucharist were called *Viatica,* because they were equally esteemed men's necessary provision and proper armour, both to sustain and conduct them safe on their way in their passage through this world to eternal life. The administration of Baptism is thus spoken of by St. Basil and Gregory Nazianzen, as the " giving to men their viaticum or provision for their journey to another world ;" and under this impression, *it was frequently delayed till the hour of death, being esteemed as a final security and safeguard to future happiness.* More strictly, however, the term *viaticum* denoted *the Eucharist given to persons in immediate danger of death, and in this sense it is still occasionally used.* The 13th Canon of the Nicene Council, ordains that none

" be deprived *of his perfect and most necessary riaticum*, when he departs out of this life." Several other canons of various councils are to the same effect, *providing also for the giving of the viaticum under peculiar circumstances, as to persons in extreme weakness*, DELIRIUM, *or subject to canonical discipline.*" (p. 562.)

Such are the " *Church Principles*" to which Dr. Hook and Mr. Palmer are committed! Upon this one subject of the Lord's Supper alone, has enough been cited to prove no little " Tendency to Romanism," in the common, ordinary and Protestant sense of the terms !— Whether such principles, such subtle distinctions, and such arguments placed in the inexperienced hands of the Students of a University, and those of our youthful divines, are, or are not calculated to furnish them with a " *Viaticum*," towards Rome, the common sense of the public must decide.

Dr. Hook's definition of " *the Catholic Church*," is worthy of notice, as differing essentially from that given in the nineteenth Article.

" Thus the Catholic Church has the Lord Christ for its founder; its prescribed form of admission is the Holy Sacrament of Baptism; its constant badge of membership is the holy Sacrament of the Eucharist; its peculiar duties are repentance, faith, obedience; its peculiar privileges, union with God, through Christ its Head, and hereby forgiveness of sins, present grace and future glory; its officers are Bishops and priests, assisted by deacons, in regular succession from the Apostles, the first constituted officers of this body corporate. It has the Bible for its code of laws, AND A DIVINE TRADITION for precedents, to aid its officers in the interpretation of that code on disputed points." (p. 143.)

What a contrast to the simple and scriptural declaration of the Article !

" The visible Church of Christ is a congregation of faithful men, in the which the pure Word of God is preached, and the sacraments be duly administered according to Christ's ordinance in all those things which of necessity are requisite to the same !"

Lengthy and minute upon some points, Dr. Hook's description of the CHURCH omits " *the preaching of the pure word of God*'—an ordinance generally thrust into the back ground by his class of Divines—but put

prominently forward in all the offices of our Protestant Church! He
inserts also " A DIVINE TRADITION," an element of the Catholic
Church, no where recognized in the *written traditions* of our own
Church. When acting up to the spirit of the first six general councils this Catholic Church is pronounced to be, if not *Infallible—" irreformable,"*—which is a term of Mr. Palmer's own creation—denoting
that which indeed has no existence! An " irreformable" " Anglo-
" Catholic Church," bears a strong resemblance *to an infallible Holy
Roman Catholic Church.*

" The doctrine of these general Councils" (says Mr. Palmer, as quoted by Dr.
Hook, p. 218) "having been approved and acted on by the whole body of the
Catholic Church, and thus ratified by an universal consent, which has continued
ever since, is *irrefragably true, unalterable, and irreformable;* nor could any
Church forsake or change the doctrine without ceasing to be Christian."

It is evident from many expressions in the volume before us that
Dr. Hook is disposed to depreciate the thirty-nine Articles, or to
esteem them, at least, as a very insufficient development of Christian
doctrine.

" It is a mistake into which ignorant persons are apt to fall, to suppose that the
Thirty-nine Articles of 1562 were intended to answer the purpose of a body of
Divinity, and it is a very grievous error for persons to speak of the Church of Eng-
land, as the Church of the Thirty-nine Articles. It is true, they contain the
decisions of the Church of England on many points of doctrine and practice; but on
others of equal importance they are silent; as on God's Providence, THE FALL OF
MAN, God's Covenants; the Rule of Christian Obedience or Obligation of the Ten
Commandments; the Law of the Sabbath, of Marriage and Divorce; the Rites of
Confirmation, Holy Orders, and other things belonging to Church government and
discipline." (p. 50.)

Those who are familar with this admirable code of Christain truth will
be not a little astonished at the boldness of the above assertions; and
it will occur to them, that in the above list of deficiencies, there are
several items which are obviously included in various articles which
might be quoted. But how will their astonishment increase when they
discover that in another page of this same work, they are referred to

the very article which contains a doctrine on which the author here affirms that the thirty-nine Articles " *are silent,*" and that one of primary and fundamental importance !

" FALL OF MAN.—The loss of those perfections and that happiness which his Maker bestowed on man at his creation, for the transgression of a positive command given for the trial of his obedience. *This doctrine may be stated in the language of our Ninth Article ! ! "* (which is then cited at length.) pp. 274, 275.

So palpable a contradiction I am at a loss to account for : and whether it discovers a bias of mind on the subject or not, I will not take upon me to decide.   At all events " Church Principles" appear to harmonize better with " *Divine Tradition*" than with the 39 Articles !

That the theory of PRAYING FOR THE DEAD, formed any part of the creed of those who are the representatives of " *Church Principles*" as contrasted with " *Romish tendencies,*" I was not prepared to discover ! But so it appears to be : and Dr. Hook shall make this remarkable confession in his own words—

" Nor yet does her (the Church's) regard for the saints departed end with their funeral.   In the prayer for the Church militant there still remains, in our Church, a *sufficient memorial* of what was still more *feelingly* expressed by the primitive Church—the interest of the surviving Christian with his departed friends,—of the Church on earth, which is militant, with the Church in hades, expectant of its triumph.   Formerly, at the Holy Eucharist, *the names of eminent saints were read aloud from the rolls of the Church, and prayers and thanksgivings were made for them, and offerings were presented on their behalf: and it is in the prayer before mentioned, which is an act of communion with all saints, coupled with an act of oblation, that the Church of England makes most express mention of the departed ;* giving thanks for them to God, who gave and hath taken away, and praying that they and we may again be blessed together.   This will appear plain, *and the connexion between the oblation and the dead will be manifest beyond dispute,* if we throw together the first and last clauses of this prayer ; thus then we pray— " Almighty and everliving God, who by Thy holy Apostle has taught us to make prayers and supplications, and to give thanks for all men ; we humbly beseech Thee most mercifully to accept our alms and oblations, and to receive these our prayers, which we offer unto Thy Divine Majesty ; beseeching Thee to inspire continually the universal Church with the spirit of truth, unity, and concord, &c.   And we also bless Thy holy name for all Thy servants departed this life in Thy faith and fear ; beseeching Thee to give us grace so to follow their good example, that with them we may be partakers of Thy heavenly kingdom."

Who would have imagined that the simple words of this prayer could have been so wrested by one of the Sons of the Protestant Church to establish a doctrine which she abhors ! This beautiful form of worship may be safely left to speak for itself—the juxta position of two of its parts, however unwarrantable, separated as they are in the original, (p. 228, 229,) cannot make it speak the voice of *Prayer for the dead.* But it is worthy of remark that this is the prayer for the restoration of which to the daily service there has recently been such a feverish anxiety in some quarters : our author endeavours to make it appear that this formulary sanctions *prayers for the dead*—and in another place as we have seen, *an oblation of an unbloody sacrifice on the Christian Altar.* Can it be that these are the peculiar charms which it presents to some eyes, and is this the language it shall be made to speak ?

The ardent sympathy of our author " *with that which was more feelingly expressed in the Primitive Church*" on this subject, leads him to still more adventurous speculations relative *to Church Discipline beyond the grave ! !* And the passage which follows will be judged by most persons to discover strong tendencies to Popery, although its ingenious and learned author endeavours to draw from it three opposite corollaries.

" As this *(as well as the yet more expressive methods of the Primitive Church,)* cannot be less than *acts of communion*, it follows that there must be something answering to that *discipline* which keeps any other part of church communion pure. Hence in our Church ' *The order for the burial of the dead*' is prefaced by a rubric which says, ' *that the office ensuing is not to be used for any that die unbaptized, or excommunicate, or have laid violent hands on themselves:*' a sentence which doubtless excludes all such persons, in the judgment of the Church, *from the act of fellowship before mentioned.* In the primitive Church a notorious offender was not enrolled on the diptychs of the Church, *(see Diptychs,)* or if enrolled before his offences were discovered, his name was struck off: *i. e. he was not remembered* in *the prayers, thanksgivings, or oblations made by the faithful.* If however this judgment of excommunication (for such in effect it was) was found afterwards to be unjust, the name of the departed was again enrolled on the diptychs ; this was the case with no less a person than St. Chrysostom.

" *And this ecclesiastical dealing with the dead will appear to answer to what is called, when the living are the subjects of it,* COMMUNION, EXCOMMUNICATION, *and* RECONCILIATION. PENANCE *and* ABSOLUTION *the nature of the case excludes.*

Thus we are taught that the Church not only enjoys communion with the souls of the departed, but exercises *ecclesiastical discipline* over them—having the power to excommunicate and to reconcile them ! Whither will these Church Principles bear us? And what unearthly powers will they confer on the Church ? Still their author affirms constantly that they will not lead us towards Rome—on the contrary, away from it ! And why ? Because the Church of Rome teaches us to pray " TO the departed Saints,'' the Primitive Church teaches us to pray " FOR them,"—" and we cannot pray TO and FOR the same persons !" Admirable system of spiritual homœopathy! Protestants are to be cured of their propensities to the invocation of saints by being taught *to pray for them !* By the same process of reasoning they are to be saved from believing in Purgatory: because the Primitive Church never prayed for the wicked, or for people in torture, " but for " those who were accounted saints *par excellence,* even including the " Blessed Virgin and the Holy Apostles," and they could not be in Purgatory ! And the third deduction is, "that works of supererogation " formed no part of the system of Primitive Theology since ALL were " prayed for"—though (our author adds with much simplicity) " IT " WAS NOT DECLARED TO WHAT PARTICULAR END !" No, indeed ! he must be learned and ingenious who can tell us " for what particular " end" prayers were thus supposed to be offered ! It is too obvious that the blessed Saints lying in the bosom of Abraham, or walking in blood-washed robes of heavenly purity, and enjoying the presence of their Lord cannot be benefited by the prayers of those trembling, sinful, weary fellow servants whom they have left behind in a world of sin and sorrow ! The doctrine is as repugnant to common sense as it is to the teaching of Holy Scripture, and the " *Church Principles*" of those who are content to draw their principles from the authorized formularies of their Protestant Church !

My readers may begin to think that enough has been adduced from the work before us to shew the author's " tendency towards Rome," although in other pages he condemns Romanism, or rather some of its tenets. But I feel it very important to multiply evidence of this nature; because it is not by one or two incautious expressions or inconsistencies that any man should be judged, or condemned; but when proof is accumulated upon many topics, all bearing on the same point, little doubt of the real sentiments of the author can remain upon a reflective mind. I shall therefore abridge Dr. Hook's opinions upon many other subjects connected with this controversy : endeavouring to abstain from remarks, although the temptation to censure is strong.

Thus, then, " *Auricular confession.*" (page 60.) " The confession " of sins at the ear of the Priest. The Romish Church not only re- " quires confession as a duty, but has advanced it to the dignity of a " Sacrament.——The error of the Romish Church consists in represent- " ing this confession as *necessary.* It is clearly shewn in Bingham, that " private confession was never deemed necessary, though *then* as *now,* " in *our own Church it was recommended !*"

And again, page 191.

" Confession.—The admission of a fault or sin. All Christians admit that we are to confess our sins to God ; but it is by many considered ' flat popery' to confess our sins to a fellow man, though that man be God's priest. Now Confession to the priest is not *commanded,* but it is in many cases *recommended,* by the Church of England : *See the warning for the celebration of the Holy Communion.*"

Whether the recommendation to a person in trouble of mind " to open his grief to some discreet and learned minister of God's word," affords the Church's sanction to " Confession of sins, to God's Priest," I will not stop to decide.

Monastic institutions, under certain regulations, and an ascetic life, are evidently sanctioned in this work.

" Monastery; a convent house built for the reception of the religious : whether it be abbey, priory, nunnery, or the like.

"Monastery is only properly applied to the houses of monks, mendicant friars, and nuns : the rest are more properly called *Religious Houses*. We have had no monasteries in our Church since the Reformation, when they were destroyed to enrich our kings and their courtiers ; but we have religious houses, such as our colleges.

"The original institution of a monastic life *was to relinquish the things of this world, and wholly to live up to the rules and precepts of our Saviour ;* but it was never intended to distinguish men by particular orders." (p. 384.)

If, therefore, we would wholly live up to the rules and precepts of our Saviour, we must return to a "*Monastic life !*"

"*But useful as monasteries had been at one time,* they were at last abused and corrupted. To such an extent had they been corrupted in the reign of Henry the VIII. that he made their corruptions a ground, not of reform, but of spoliation. The property of the monasteries was seized in the reign of this monarch, and that of his successor, and given to their courtiers. Much of the property which was once employed in supporting learned men of humble birth, and might be still so employed, is now expended in purposes wholly alien to the intention of the original grantees." —*See Impropriator.*

It is evident that our author parts with *monasteries* with a sigh.

We now approach a variety of superstitious usages, sanctioned indeed, in whole or in part by what Dr. Hook calls the "*Primitive Church*," that is, not the *Apostolic Church*, as she subsisted before the canon of Scripture was closed—but the Church of that dark and dismal period which immediately succeeded the death of the last of the Apostles ; respecting which our information is scanty and imperfect, but by whose dim and uncertain light these divines would have us walk, in preference to the broad day-light of Holy Scripture. I am well aware that in exposing these usages and protesting against them, I shall involve myself in the charge of "*Ultra-Protestantism*," at least in the judgment of the author of the "Church Dictionary" and his associates—it may be of *Latitudinarianism !* But it is a satisfaction to find myself in good company : as appears from page 343,—

"LATITUDINARIANS.—Certain divines so called from the latitude of their principles, the term is chiefly applied to some divines of the 17th century, such as

Hales, *Chillingworth*, Whichcot, *Tillotson*, *Burnet*. These men were attached to the English establishment, as such, but regarded episcopacy, and forms of public worship as among the things indifferent. They would not exclude from their communion those who differed from them in those particulars. *Many of the Latitudinarian divines commenced as Calvinists and ended as Socinians.*"

Of course I write my protest against such a disingenuous insinuation as the above!

As specimens of *superstitious usages* approved by Dr. H. I cite the following :   Five pages are occupied in arguing the propriety of—

"LIGHTS ON THE ALTAR.—Among the ornaments of the Church enjoined by the laws, and sanctioned by the usage, in the Church of England, are two lights upon the altar, to be a symbol to the people that Christ, in His two-fold nature, is the very true Light of the world." (p. 356.)

"The laws of the Church" respecting candles thus dogmatically propounded, rest solely upon an inference drawn from an injunction of Ed. VI. The Rubric enjoins that "Church ornaments," &c. shall in other respects, remain the same as in the 2d year of Ed. VI. An injunction of the 6th Ed. is then produced, which decrees that all torches, tapers, candles, &c. shall be removed from the churches except " two lights only on the HIGH ALTAR, before the Sacrament."

Some one has ventured to suggest that we have no "*High Altar*" now, and that therefore the injunction is inapplicable: but he is branded by Dr. Hook with " ignorance of History"—the fact being " that the *High Altar* alone is left in our churches, all the rest being " removed by Authority"! The custom of the church is shewn by the *practice* still retained in Collegiate Chapels, and Chapels Royal, &c. The removal of these symbolic candles is attributed not to the Reformers but to the Puritans—these lights are vindicated as primitive, as beautiful emblems—as alluded to in the seven candlesticks of the Revelation— the various numbers of them adopted in the different churches have all appropriate symbolic meanings—even to the 70,000 candles burning at one time in St. Peter's at Rome—" the number two, which is *specially*

" *Anglican*, refers DOUBTLESS, to the two natures of Christ, in which he " is especially the very true light of the world"!! p. 356, 361. On the same subject, we have the following—

" CANDLEMAS DAY.—A name formerly given to the festival of the Purification of the Virgin Mary, observed in our Church, February 2. *In the ancient Church,*" (and therefore the correct Church), " this day was remarkable for the number of lighted candles, which were borne about in processions, and placed in churches, in memory of Him who came to be ' a light to lighten the Gentiles, and the glory of His people Israel.' From this custom the name is supposed to be derived."

All this may be primitive, may be the genuine fruits of such " Church Principles"—but we may surely demur upon their propriety without being considered " Ultra-Protestants."

Croziers, crosses, and various emblematic ornaments in Churches, and offices are earnestly contended for. The Bishops are at once censured and excused for neglecting a Rubric *still in force* in the prayer book of the 2d of Ed. VI.—they celebrate the communion without " *their Pastoral Staff* in their hands!!"

" The writer of this article does not remember to have seen an English Bishop attired as this rubric directs. Most, if not all of the Bishops probably omit this observance in condescension to the superstition of those whose consciences, though *not offended at a transgression of a command of the Church*, might be offended at ornaments which many pious persons reverence as emblematical." (p. 220.)

Another reason might be suggested for this Episcopal omission, viz.: that perhaps our venerable Pastors might think the custom itself tended to superstition, and therefore they dropped it! Dr. Hook constantly applies the term *superstition* to the conscientious feelings of Protestants —the term is not very appropriate nor is the suggestion with which it is accompanied very charitable.

" CROSS.—The sign of the Cross was made in the PRIMITIVE CHURCH in some part of almost every Christian office. In the Church of England it is commanded to be used only in the Sacrament of Baptism * * * and PERHAPS in the Sacrament of the Eucharist, where it *may be implied* in the direction that the Priest shall lay his hand on the bread and wine when he consecrates them!" (pp. 220, 221.)

Great must be the attachment to this usage in the mind of him who could discover it in such a direction of the Church ! Then follows a lengthened argument in favour of erecting Crosses on every sanctuary —" and on every altar whereon the sacrifice of the crucified is commemorated."

" Why should we admit into our Churches *the lion and the unicorn, and yet banish the cross?* Why head our processions with flags and colours denoting political partizanship, and giving rise to angry political feeling, and leave it to Romish dissenters to bear before them the cross, the badge of Christianity ?"

Why ? Because "*the Lion and the Unicorn*" form part of the Royal Arms, which every lover of the Union between Church and State would wish to see exhibited in all our Parish Churches even if there were not an express injunction on the subject !—Why ? Because we never heard of the Lion and Unicorn leading to superstitious usages—and the emblem of the cross has been fruitful in idolatry ! The one is enacted by the Powers that be—and the other receives no sanction in our canons and offices. But the task of wading through the petty superstitions of this book is wearisome and endless. I must only allege them and leave the reader to refer to the particular passages. " BOWING TO THE ALTAR—is a reverend custom still practised at " Windsor Chapel, in College Chapels and Cathedrals." (p. 102.) " STREWING WITH FLOWERS—is a very simple and most innocent " method of ornamenting the Christian Altar." (p. 283.) The use of " HOLY WATER" "*blessed with an appropriate service by the priest,*" is evidently mentioned as a thing approved—and only " obliged to be " discontinued at the Reformation" because " so many superstitions " had become connected with it." (p. 306.) " IMMERSION—is the " proper mode of administering the Sacrament of Baptism, *by which* " *first the right side, then the left, then the face are dipped in the font.*" The author does not give his authority for this peculiar method of baptizing. " The Antient Christians placed the Altar on the East, " so that in facing towards the Altar in their devotions they turned " to the East." (p. 246.) The cruel ORDEAL OF FIRE, water, red hot plough-shares, and other barbarous tests to which accused persons were put, in a dark and superstitious age, in order to discover their guilt, or prove their innocence, is described at considerable length, and dismissed without a single censure! The following clause seems rather to indicate belief in these false miracles than otherwise.

" The Christians of this age had a strong reliance upon this way of trial, not in the least doubting but that God would suspend the force of nature, and clear the truth by a supernatural interposition. If we may believe the records of those times, we shall find that innocent persons were frequently rescued in a surprising manner." (p. 407.)

In the same superstitious strain is the following—" DEMONIACS : " Persons possessed of the devil. For the cure of such persons there " were peculiar services in the PRIMITIVE CHURCH. They are now all " of them treated as Lunatics." page 237. The Royal miracle of curing the KING'S-EVIL, supposed to have been hereditary in the Kings of England and France, is thus treated of :—

" The whole subject of the truth or falsehood of these pretensions is confessedly ' one of difficulty, *but all evidence is certainly in favour of their truth ;* and it is clearly more probable that we should be *absurdly incredulous*, than that all genera- tions, for many ages should be deceived in a matter before their eyes !" (354, 355.)

The *service* used at the " *time of touching*," is then subjoined.— " MORALITIES, MYSTERIES, and MIRACLES,—a kind of theatrical " representations, which were made by the Monks and Friars, and " other ecclesiastics of the middle ages, *the vehicle of instruction to the* " *people !*" (page 393.) These profane, and often polluting mimers are rather applauded than condemned! " A high tone of *morality* was often apparent in them"—and they were "sometimes the vehicle of *positive Theology*." Under the word " DEDICATION" (234, 235) various feasts and wakes are commended. "This *laudable custom* of " wakes prevailed for many ages, till the Puritans began to exclaim " against them as a remnant of Popery." Bishop Laud is cited as vindicating and re-establishing them. Many particulars are detailed, the various dresses of the priests, the processions with lighted candles, in the primitive Church. (p. 234) Preaching in the surplice is affirmed to be the most correct.—" EMBLEMS" (p. 254) as the trine compass, or the " circle inscribed within an equilateral triangle" (denoting the Trinity) " the hand extended from the clouds—*for the* " *first person in the Trinity*—the Lamb triumphant—the fish—the " pelican—the *phœnix rising from the flames* for the resurrection—the " cross—the crown—all these are beautifully significant, *and are* " *very innocent in their use, as well as pious in their intention.*" The primitive kiss, by the circulation of the " Pax" is commended—p. 430, and the " Piscina," (440) and " Penance," (431.) And the " *Stabat Mater*," one of the " *Prosæ*" or hymns of the Roman church, is named as "*beautiful*," while no notice is taken of the most idolatrous invocations of the Virgin Mary, which it contains. I might cite much language as evidently hostile to *Protestantism*, as all this is favourable to *Popery*.

But I forbear. The task which I have undertaken is far from pleasant to me : a sense of duty alone has induced me to attempt it. A mere glance through the pages of this " Church Dictionary," convinced me that if these were "*the Church Principles*" of Mr. Palmer (and he has identified himself with them,) the attempt to rescue them from the charge of *a Romish tendency*, was hopeless—that it was only necessary to make them generally known, and all unprejudiced persons must see their affinity with all that full-grown Romanism which Mr. Palmer has so justly exposed in his recent pamphlet.

Dr. Hook rightly traces the greater portion of these superstitions to the Church of the third and fourth centuries: such were the seeds then sown, and the harvest they yielded may be contemplated in the mediæval and subsequent ages. The Romanism of the Council of Trent is but the wide spread tree of which the seed was deposited in the early ages. The same seeds will always produce the same fruits : bury them a hundred feet deep in the earth, and up-turn them after the lapse of centuries, and the process of vegetation will give the same results. Thus the seeds of ancient superstition have been sown by Mr. Palmer and his associates on the banks of the Isis, and the secessions to Rome, and all the follies of the younger clergy in the present day, are the natural and immediate fruits which they have yielded. Again I acquit these respectable writers of any intention to betray their church to Romanism—*they are deceived by their own principles.* "But men do not gather grapes of thorns, nor figs of "thistles." "A good tree cannot produce evil fruit, nor an evil tree "good fruit;" and therefore unless the divine and unerring test of nature and of nature's God is to become a fallacious guide—unless "a tree is no longer to be known by its fruits"—the "*Church Principles*" of Mr. Palmer—of Dr. Hook, and the class whom they represent, contain the germs of all the poisonous and bitter fruits which they now themselves bewail!

And if this be so—what must be the *nature and tendency* of "*the Church Principles*" of that residue of the party from whom Mr. Palmer appears now to be partially dissevered? They can be nothing but direct *Romish Principles*—though held alas! by many who still call themselves members of the British Protestant Church, and even of her Priesthood! We doubt not that as the consciences of these erring brethren become awakened to the nature of the false position which they occupy, they will drop off one by one to the see of Rome, as many have already done. And if they refuse to retract their errors, the safety of the Church and a regard for the integrity of public principle, must prevent any regret (but for their own sakes) at their departure.

And now dismissing the peculiarities of the "Church Principles" of Mr. Palmer and Dr. Hook, I would offer a few parting observations upon "Church Principles" generally. This term as too often used, is a mere cant expression—an undefined inappropriate phrase, comprising an extensive *sliding scale* of doctrine and discipline, of which the private opinion of the person who speaks is the regulating medium. So that in fact "Church Principles" in the lips of most persons, mean nothing more than "My *principles* on Church matters!" And the phrase is generally hurled at some other person whose views are supposed to be lower down the scale than those of the former. The expression forms a substitution for the now old fashioned word *orthodox,* which in its day bore much the same indefinite import. Are there then, it may be asked, no sound "Church Principles"—in other words, no scriptural principles on which the doctrines and discipline of the Christian Church are founded ? Undoubtedly there are ! And they are exhibited not in an isolated canon, or neglected rubric, much less in the writings of the third and fourth centuries, but in the general sense and system expounded in the thirty-nine Articles, the Creeds, and Liturgy of our beloved Church!   Here are my " Church Principles !" and I would know no others !   And in these I look in vain for the unmeasured condemnation of unepiscopal Churches—for the necessity of Apostolic descent to enable a minister to make a valid sacrament ; for those exaggerated and self-important dogmas, which appear now to be adopted even by some otherwise enlightened and pious evangelists ! For such persons I especially tremble; believing that extravagantly high Church notions cannot long be held by any faithful man without casting over his ministry a cold mist, which chills every statement of gospel truth—and confuses the minds of his people. " Church Principles" *as generally understood,* have little affinity to Gospel principles ; they are as Saul's armour to David, an incumbrance rather than a defence; and simple Gospel truth, as the shepherd boy's sling and stone, often proves more powerful even against the Giant Schism itself than all the boasted and elaborate armoury of Church councils, decrees, injunctions, and traditions !

𝔉inis.

J. J. HADLEY, Printer, Journal Office, Cheltenham.